Rob Bartlitz

1

Tales of Woros: Book 1

Reytan

Dedicated to the memory of my aunt

Margaret, who inspired me to read

avidly from a very early age...

Table of Contents

Prologue

The hills were barren and bare
And the cattle grazed beneath;
Sheep with nowt to wear,
Softly spread across the heath,

Were weeping in their sorrow
Of remaining in their beds
Until time had wreathed a barrow
With carcasses of late-dead

And the young who'd not survive
While vulpine fiends flickered
Their flash-light eyes like knives
From Stygian dykes of thicket,

Luring strangers in the void
Where no jewel would bestir
But caitiffs, busy in their ploy -
Drooling blood onto their fur.

Such was air of acrid taste
Reeking up the crooked roots,
Twisted in their will to chaste
The earthen rock's forbidden fruits;

Such was time of morsel mirth,
Crooning treetops, and the stench
Of dying birth,
A sneer in the face of its maternal wench.

Here 'twas that fiery men
Burned their odious breath,
Crippled words and then -
Faced death;

Here 'twas that babies cried
Prickled by the thorns of roses, blind,
Bedevilled by the snide
Hatred of those left behind;

Here, in the hideous lakes
That drowned the larks and the holly
Sleeps eternity whose oily fakes,
Decked in wreaths of folly,

Pine in anger of days past,
Diseased in every grain,
When iniquity and disgust
Were craved like lust and bane;

Misfortune, uncovered and irate,
Had touched upon this glade
Till creepy-fingered fate,
Recovering from its shade,

Engendered filth so
Bare as none before
Had seen or smelt, that blowed
East at speeds of air or more,

And crippled every smoke ring
That there be:
A miserly king
In the kingdom of misery,

The last gash of a sword
In the body of a dead,
The Judas who poured
Poisoned wine with bread,

Death itself,
Though dull and grey,
Unstained, with verve
Commenced that day,

The day that none'll forget.

Day One

The lustre of the heavens
Waned till Sun was bare,
And the nightly frolics, deadened,
Froze in sultry air,

With their deposed lunar emperor
Sleeping soundly,
Flawlessly temporal,
Sunken in the ground;

Vagrant chalice-bearers
Were now knocking on ebony doors,
Selling creepy-berries
To get ready for the coming of bubonic wars,

And pestilence of blight,
And every other nature's plaintive cry
That with surplus slight
Caused many a creature to die;

Fishermen with shaven noses,
Surrounded with filial piety
And skeleton roses
That marked the borders of their society,

Were sipping icy ales
In the misty, dripping caves,
Gathering dirt behind their nails,
Digging graves,

Knitting yarns of valiant fathers
Who, like them, were
Minstrels to the cause of others,
And everywhere

Was bloody childbirth,
Rogues, knaves, boors
Whose feet kicked the earth
In search of forgotten cures,

Charlatans, fakes,
Masters of phoney pretence,
Heroic mistakes,
Sceptics of rational sense,

Spiteful kings,
Knights with dreams,
And jesters with wings
Whose pageantry and means

Strangled a noble few
Who'd fawn upon the royalty
In the name of their brew,
Under the name of loyalty.

Thus the monarch was barren,
And his people were bare,
With no comfort to hide 'em
But the westerly waves of air

That kept them so warm
During the long days of summer
When vermin was born
In the fields of roebuck and grannom.

And the heat of the Sun
Ignited the carcass heap
Of dead sheep till there was only one
Left for to share and eat…

But the eyes of the land
This morn were ne'er shut,
For yestreen - the lunar sands
Were seen to be torn like the wings of a bat,

And the people were wary,
So the children were fed on
The chalice-bearers' berries
To protect them from the Armageddon;

And huts were built
From salmon tails,
Padded with quilt
And worn-out sails,

Decked in objects of deity
Which they usually kept
Strapped to their rickety
Limbs. There they slept

With one eye shut
And the other wide awake
Till noon, when every single hut
Began to slowly shake.

Men cried with silence
And women stabbed their breasts,
Fearing cruel violence
That high winds from the west

Always bring.
And it was then that some heard
The beating of the wing
And the screech of the bird

That they came to dread
From this day onward,
For every time its ugly head
Appeared from the woods,

The land was ravaged
And roots were torn
From earth's crust, and savage
Rains of Abaddon

Swept through treeless moors
Like blinded wrath of gods.
First time, it came to soar
Above where roe deer trod,

Then with a human yell
It dropped onto the carcass heap,
And the air began to smell,
And the sky began to weep.

For an hour or more
The tempest was rife;
Trees were thrown in war
With last bastions of life,

Clouds, stretched beyond horizon,
Stabbed fiercely with their light
Where the Eagle of Demise on
Carcass-meat dined with such delight;

Fires burned the villages,
And drowned the ashes,
Then buried the villagers
Whose bloodless gashes

Oozed pain,
And the anger that threatened to plough the
stockade
Where remnants of grain
From winter's futile trade

Rotted. At long last,
When dust finally settled
On the fetid pus
Of the stinging Apollyon Nettle,

A faint, but sordid howl
Echoed through the arid sands,
And the wide-eyed screeching fowl
Of the nether land

Flew with a mocking air
Towards its hispid nest,
On a mountain bare,
In the gargoyle, sinuous west.

The silence that followed
Was long and cold,
Timeless and hollow
Like the churchyard vault,

Solid and dead
Like the tombstone of the Maker,
Which once bled
Prior to breaking

Under the strain
Of callous guile
When watchmen and sextons did entertain
With parasite smiles

That were forgotten on Sundays.
Oh, how mighty the awe,
The glory and the grace
Of nature's law,

The zenith and the nadir,
The root and the style
Of God's treason, that here
Was now festering in bile:

The dead cardinal's limbs,
The smoky hair of mortis rigor,
The priestess's forbidden dreams
Of marrying her grave-digger,

The organist's malice,
The king's pet weeds,
A chalice-bearer's chalice -
All have now borne their seeds.

And the priest who crept up
With his howling iron tongue,
Had vainly swallowed up
His blood-filled ailed lung,

For the knight-errantry that he showed
Was foolish now,
Not bold;
And as his body lay in sour

Filth, at putrid rest,
A fathomless chasm,
In naked savagery dressed,
With ashen miasma

Seething at its vent,
Sucked it in with ogreish breath,
Rendering the corpulent
Father wheezing whiffs of death.

A bestial deluge of fire
Then swept the through the cordial lake
To burst onto the quagmire
Where the sleeping snakes

Bedded their young,
And with one flash of light
Stabbed the living lung,
Spawning nightmares at the dawn of night.

And still as mighty dark could be
When crippled by celestial rakes,
In its fields and holts of misery
Beacon eyes where all that stayed awake.

Day Two

The warm, gin-wet
Grass, with surplice wash,
Damp cloister fret,
And shade for to quash

The airs of dudgeon
Now healing in the forge
Where curates poured their blood on
Guards of the bastion gorge,

Became a pedlar's morgue
Of razor nails, accordion rags,
Itinerant wraiths and rogues,
Marly bones and stags.

And the creek where the frenzied waters
Once had crumbled solid boulders,
Smelt of sour, jaundiced, hot air,
As it rested on its sunken shoulders.

The king, who was of mongrel breed,
Perused the knight for assurance
Whom trusted he in every deed
And shared his every abhorrence.

The armour, though beaten and vile,
Straightened in one specious twitch;
Thence, with a mind not short of deviant
guile
Made attempt at an ingratiating speech,

And as of ample anatomy was he
And famed for his repute,
Listened the king with glee
To the grovelling brute.

The jester sneered at this wile
And breathed a heavy air;
His teeth, stained with yellow bile,
Chewed on soily hair

That crept from underneath an old motley-
hood
Down to the shabby black woollen cloak:
The only tokens of his livelihood.
And when the knight had spoke,

The scornful eyes of the royal fool
Sneered at his conceited master,
Pinched at his cloak of wool,

And in a mien fit only for jesters,

Bowed his head below the knees
Where he stayed till pain was showing.
By then the news had spread like disease
And soon, every ageing

Casuist who bore the badge of Themis
Was calling for the hearse-
Monger to be brought upon the premises
To face punishment far worse

Than even the fiercest
Gods would pucker their brow
At; but the minds of such men invest
In deeds most foul,

If it fit their purpose.
Thus he was rashly summoned,
And so, carried in fetters
Under the grimly command

Of the fatuous knight,
Lacerated at the shoulders,
A design to bate his might;
Anger smouldering

From underneath a big black mop of
withered hair,
And tethered he was to a

26

Martyr post, where
They smeared him with ordure.

Amongst the deadly nightshade
A crooked mile away,
A pair of hollow eyes, like blades,
Was piercing the festered air…

Not now, not then,
But ever timeless the beat
Of the heart is when
Meat eats meat;

Power's sacred
When it is to win,
The jester knew that
And he did grin.

Of ignoble birth he was conceived
Destined to serve the higher echelons,
Reytan they called him, and he agreed,
'Twas a name he would depend on.

Many a year he spent at the court,
Watching the wheels fall off the king's cart,
The Knight was his enemy, the man who
could thwart
Every desire he had at his heart.

The royal hearse-monger got under the feet

Of both Reytan's and The Knight's
ambitions,
So they conspired to serve defeat,
His perpetual wink for 'em was a welcome
addition.

The jester's orb now got smaller by one,
Yet t'was still a dark heavy mass,
And right at the top, sat one crackbrained
man,
The boor and the lout that was King Sass.

Day Three

A horrid stench of amanita brew
Filled the royal court from end to end
As the king, who
Invited friends

For dinner, was preparing to be clad
In most expensive garb;
And in the grounds below, the blood
Of men-at-arms, in bards,

Was boiling in the sweltering heat.
This morning the news of the feast
Were read out to the beat
Of a drum by a priest,

So the people were now
Gathering in the square,
Ready to kowtow
To the nobles that these were –

Far removed from common touch,
Lost in their eternal bliss,
Seldom seen, hated much,
Pompous, putrid, pious piss.

In the musty hollowness
Of king's bed chamber
Reytan's heartless sunken chest
In black dressed; a deadly spectre

Moulded to the creaking throne through
wile,
Not honour or fidelity;
A foul-smelling shyster, beguiler,
Sewer-rat in finery;

His creepy, tenuous fingers
Locked like shackles in his lap,
Pointed, greased and blackened chin hair,
Face like soiled map.

There - two diamonds where the
Treasure of his brain
Shone through cloudy weather
Of the royalty's disdain.

And the choking clouds of dust
That filled the empty room
From mahogany rot to pillow crust:
They're solace to his gloom.

A hall thus full of ghostly fate,
Only recent raged their fun,
Some had realised, but too late,
For the deed, it now was done.

'Twas a long stroll then he took
Down the hallway to the end
Where sat waiting for this crook
Was King Sass, no creature's friend.

The tall dark wooden doors
Creaked wide open to reveal
Reytan's madness, in control,
To the king's Achilles heel.

Next to him in rusted metal
Stood The Knight like peacock-he,
Proud to be in such fine fettle,
Ready to drop to his knee.

Sass spoke slowly with a sneer:
"Reytan, tell me, 'tis the end?"
Jester bowed, "victory's near,
No more shalt thou fear thy friends."

The wind had howled outside the gates,
Cold were words that brought this news,
But he who fears is he who hates,
An ever easier path to choose.

Day Four

A blustery fog had set on Woros,
The land where everyman was blind,
You could hear the dulled hum of sorrow
Screaming through each troubled mind;

Trees were groaning with love's pain
That not a single soul had e'er met,
For the gentleness of cupid's reign
Had long abandoned here with regret.

Sweeping through this desolation,
Waves of avarice guised as progress
Made design upon this nation
Whence by priesthood could be blest;

No one spoke much, 'twas not needed
Every morbid day the same,
But not this morn, which they heeded,
A day it was in just the name;

Darkness lingered far too long,
And men were growing mighty sore,
Doom was palpable, as it blowed strong
'Cross the blackened woodland floor.

Some swore they could almost see
A shadow sweeping through the clouds;
Piercing eyes of destiny
Shone upon them, they cried loud.

But nothing doing, silence still,
All seemed calm within the reservoir,
Till one tearful moment, when this stillness
filled
With a distant roar coming from afar.

The ground it trembled with much dread,
Voices tore through subdued grief,
No soul knew what they just heard,
Only feet felt fear beneath;

Slow the rumble was, but steady
As the increase of their breath,
Lips spoke nowt, but they were ready,
So resigned were to their deaths.

Then the might of water's edge
Swiftly swelled onto dry land,
Rivers broke and launched to dredge
The muddy swill into their hands;

Icons of protector saints
Flowed like leaves through torrid waters,
Bodies of frail priests, reticent,
Followed blind into the slaughter.

Damn those good men in their minds,
Flying high above the waves of sin;
The Knight was too one of their kind,
Finest sample Sass had seen.

King and he had gathered council,
The best raw brains in kingdom's realm,
Spoke each one within the houseful
As the ass sat proudly at the helm;

Long were yarns of former glory
Every dullard here declared,
Noble was each specious story
While the torrent claimed more dead.

Finally, 'twas The Knight's turn.
He broke ranks and faced the sky;
Awkward silence he thus earned,
And when he spoke, he spoke dry:

"If thy highness shall grant wish,
I will take my bravest brothers,
Send 'em to the hell's abyss
To repel the water's lathers.

These great men have not met fear,
Nor they ever query orders;
Allow me to set them free with spears -
They shall form robust borders."

Sass's trust in this buffoon
Meant no questions begged to ask,
"Go, my friend, do it soon,
Hie about thy solid task."

So the best and the strongest
From across the land had mustered,
Given they were strictest orders
From this simple knight, their master;

Each one swore to their own idol,
Cries of "Anhur!", "Maahes!" too,
Water's softly whispered tidals
Beckoned the fools' army through;

Charge they did in their masses,
Thousands more behind them ran,
No one fathomed who was fastest -
Horsed brigades or orphaned men;

Battle raged between these Spartans
And the nature's ebb and flow,
Down they went, ne'er disheartened,
While their confidence did grow;

Every chest bowed out in honour
To the magna parva of King Sass,
Shields engraved with Saint Monan,
Martyr of the High Alsace;

Spears, axes, maces, daggers,
Swords and lances, scythes and flails,
All were thrown with murderous swagger -
Every effort doomed to fail.

High above this sorry din,
A pair of eyes so dark but shrewd
Watched these merchants of all sin
Drown like ants in bat's blood stew;

The shriek it gave could not be heard
Above the noise of dying champions,
So flew away the crooked bird
To nest within its moss campion.

By then, the slaughter was complete,
And while the water's edge moved not a
foot,
Sass's army was depleted,
Every helmet, every boot.

Thousand widows lined the gates
In the sordid aftermath,
Rivers faded hours later,
Bored of their erst wrath.

She'd make all her garments
Out of its rancid rough pelt,
For she said no one would harm her
If they knew how death smelt.

And as her oily hair floated feral
In the misty heaviness of air,
Suddenly, she heard a thud of peril
Galloping down the thoroughfare;

Friend or enemy? Not so clear,
Reytan was upon a stolen steed,
Moved she hair off of her ear,
Come he'd only in his need.

She sneered at how unwieldy
Site was this she came to spy,
Clutching at her sword, unyielding,
Would he live or would he die?

History 'tween them it was mottled,
Many times he would excel
At wickedness that no mere mortal
Could do when doing himself.

Wary was she of this cad
Ever since the eve they met,
Reytan's sin was not in mad-
Ness, but to always be disconsolate;

Crooked stature with a mien
Of shaman's doll in tatters,
Soulless eyes, pained faux grin,
Every phrase aimed to flatter.

Slightly bowed he thus proceeded,
To Aurelia's side he lumbered,
Motion that was far from needed
For she knew him and his number.

"Do I serve thee hemlock wine
Or a nettle confit stew?
Will you waste my precious time
Or is something here for you?"

"Fine Aurelia, thou are sweet
E'er so humble and demure
Throw myself right at thy feet,
Love for which I have no cure."

"Nuff obsequiousness, I am no fool,
Though yourself you claim to be,
'Tis my land, and thus my rules,
What's your need?", hollered she.

Reytan twisted his pate up
While his mouth gave half a grin,
"Nettle confit stew, one cup,
Perilous journey mine hath been."

"Death I cannot him bestow
For the king will simply mourn,
Fear and mistrust's harder blows
Out of falsehoods must be borne."

The jester's smile widened somewhat,
Satisfying were the words she said,
Through machinations of the harlot
Now to him The Knight was dead.

Just as his heart pounded
With the vile beat of her scheme,
Heard he but a faint sound,
Weak and humble, yet obscene.

"What from Hades is that, tell,
Which can make my pale skin crawl?"
"Nothing wicked, not from hell,
Nothing evil 'tis at all;

Change your subject not with me,
All my deeds they must be earned;
Still you have not furnished me
With what I will have in return."

Reytan blowed a puff of air,
Closer he got to her space,
Slowly answered he to her,
Speaking firmly in her face:

It had not been best of nights,
Yet 'twas bathed in peaceful glory,
Broken up by firelights -
Blessed cathartic purgatory.

To the royal palace hill
Came a messenger from far,
Haunting yellow at the gills,
Face more red then cinnabar;

"Grant me audience with thy king",
Begged he at the iron gates,
"Vital news to him I bring
That entail the fate of states."

Brought he was up to the throne
Where King Sass was soundly sleeping,
Woke he with impatient groan,
Stretching jaw till it was creaking.

Clicked his fingers for The Knight
To be summoned from his rest;
Wanted he him by his side,
Feeling certain this was best.

Finally, when all present were,
Sass then gestured at the runner
Making plain he did not care
For such urgency of manner.

Messenger, though weak and frail,
Bent down to the floor in pain:
"Hark, your honour, lest I fail,
Sombre presage most insane

Here I give you in these words:
Please avert the war that brews
'Tween the ruthless Vilaherts
And the peoples that serve you.

Tribe this knows of the misfortunes
That befell your realm of late,
Soldiers they all are of fortune,
Full of greed for what they hate.

Send me they did to your knees
To propose a deal you might
Here consider, beg you please,
And avoid a losing fight.

Give them passage through the creek
Where no weeds had dared to spawn,
Of no use to you this bleak
Gorge is, that you must have known;

They will bother you no more,
Pillage, rape will be of past,
Weary they are of its gore,
Weapons they will down at last."

Reytan, hunched and pensive in his manner,
Seated close to royal limb,
Peered up through his wary rancour,
Pinching his own bloodless skin,

Begged he with his hollow eyes
For the king to not be quick,
Formulate an answer wisely,
Not to make the impasse sick.

But Sass's boredom could be felt
From the entrance to the pew
Where imperial guards had knelt,
Since the deluge - only few.

"Threat it is, and I'm not used
To bending down to such lows;
Tell your masters that their ruse
Was defective, much like every beggar's
clothes;

Woros is the realm exemplar
To all kingdoms through the land,
Piteous and sad all attempts are
To demean its denizens;

Strong our bloodlines and our valour,
Every other lives in fear,
Death to all their deathly pallor,
Should they ever dare to near.

And no deal will I observe,
Beg for mercy they will too,
Such pomposity, oh, such nerve
Thinking they will make me do."

"I will deal with this, my sir."
Broke The Knight his master's speech.
"Let me take the messenger,
Admonition I shall teach."

Metal clunked as The Knight
Took the delegate, enthused,
Beaming with untold delight
That he made the king amused.

"Army's weak", Reytan whispered
As the room was filled with two,
"No one's stratagem tastes crispier
Than when it is thought through."

"Wise you are, I have no doubt."
Answered Sass as if in thought.
"Weakness I cannot act out
When a knave's ear's taut.

I shall charge my brave Sir Knight
With amassing a new horde
To protect our every right
With the heaviest might of sword."

Reytan knew when to stop,
The seeds of doubt must not be thrown,
Planted better, so a crop
Of parasites is borne.

Left him he did in that chamber
Of perfidious royal bubble,
As the clunking had got fainter,
Jester knew that it spelled trouble.

This ship of fools, this Jonah's vessel,
Beached itself on dunes of folly;
Catastrophe of good intentions nestle
In the darkest melancholy.

A breach of trust at every turn,
An air of failure with each breath,
Nothing's sacred, nothing's earned,
You are born to wait till death.

As the evening begged to close
With the pitch-dark sky severe,
Reytan followed his own shadow
Up to higher atmosphere;

At the mountain top of sable,
Where the ravens come to rest,
He peered out as he was able
And pricked ears he could best;

High above the vale of rain,
Hanging off a half-dead log,
Was the messenger in chains,
In a gibbet cage, in fog.

Faint and haunting was the cry
Emanating from his lips,
Echoing ghoul-like through the sky,
A macabre soul eclipse.

Vilaherts had steadily rallied
At the far-off barbican,
Seven hundred at last tally -
This has always been their plan.

Day Seven

Far and wide across the land
Candle lights grew ever dimmer,
Pallid sheets of winter's fan
Blew the ground dust even thinner;

Pointy skeletons of trees,
Last remains of living ghosts,
In their death throws on their knees,
All was dying coast to coast.

On a hill beneath the Moon
That was waning back to ground,
On the frosted silver dune
Stood Perfidio with no sound.

Eyebrows black above blue eyes,
Chest like bulwark of cruel glee,
Jaw that spoke to hypnotise,
In black metal clad was he.

Next to him in fierce red,
Scararossa, his right-hand,
Vicious, mad, compassion dead,
Agitator firebrand.

In the vale right there before them,
Fields of squalor and of penury,
Broken minions, stagnant golems,
Begging to neglect all memory.

Sorry was this sight to even
Heartless merchants of foul slaughter,
Like Perfidio, nature's demon,
Hardened villain and a rotter.

Lifted up his left hand he did,
Scararossa got the sign,
Both then mounted their wild steeds
Perfect evil, yet divine.

As his right hand swept before him,
Scararossa bolted swiftly
With a madman's pointless grin
And a band of hundred fifty.

All along the wooded hills,
Huts were lighting up the sky,
Torching those that weren't first killed,
Hoping they'd be next to die.

Rugged, stinking Vilaherts
Spread such dread where'er they rode,
People screamed, but not with words,
Fear maimed more than the sword.

And amongst this disarray
Flash of crimson could be seen
Jolting to and fro in melee,
In a bloodlust most obscene.

Many times throughout the dusk,
Silence followed every pelt,
Only for an even bloodier thrust
To another hut be dealt.

One by one along the edge,
Holts and villages they fell down
To the mighty cutting edge
Of the red-clothed rabid hound.

Meanwhile, in the courtyard proper,
Dressed in perfect white, The Knight
Lined up troops of shanghaied paupers
Whom he dressed in whiter white.

"Heroes you are", he announced.
"Men of valour, strength and courage.
Enemy will dare not pounce
When they've faced your valiant barrage.

History will remember this,
How you stood up for things righteous
Pain is victory, death is bliss,
Cowardice shall never smite us.

Go, my men, brave liberators,
War awaits your hungry swords,
Beating hearts of these frail raiders
You will bring to me in droves.

Your King Sass sits in his tower
Where he holds the finest view
Of this land's distinguished power
In the rank and file that's you.

You will make him proud today,
For there is no greater decency
Than to give your life away
For his living deity."

And upon closing his speech,
Bade them all farewell he did,
Through the gates they rode out, each
Clutching at his own white steed.

In the tower high above,
Sass was placid in his mien,
Peering like a hunting dove
Down onto this grizzly scene.

Reytan knew this was sheer madness,
So he stayed down in the war room,
With a face that glowed with sadness
And an air of doom before him.

"Damned Aurelia, where's her succour?"
Thoughts had clouded his sharp brain,
"One fine useless saboteur
She's when status quo's the same.

The Knight will singlehandedly destroy
All that Woros ever had,
And so pointless is my ploy
If The Knight is not yet dead."

And as Reytan slammed his fury
On the table with his fist,
Nature's cruellest judge and jury
Raged outside within the mist.

Crowds of white-robed, terrified
Men were shivering like lost souls,
Knowing they were there to fight
Scararossa's army ghosts.

And this haze and fog of war
Billowing wide across the open fields
Then surrounded them and more,
Right up to their wooden shields.

Quiet followed, e'er more solemn,
Winds had slowed down too right then;
No one spoke for one long moment,
Calm that followed - inhumane.

Stillness through eternity flowed,
Pounding hearts and bated breaths
Slowly turned so dark and cold
While every man awaited death.

Every eye turned to its side,
Beads of sweat formed crusty ice,
There was nowhere here to hide,
Hell's a door to paradise.

Just then, somewhere in the corner
Of the circle they had made,
Someone heard a muffled warning
And saw a glistening of a blade.

A faint thud, brutally hollow,
Took a soldier right off-kilter,
Murky wickedness had swallowed
One into the depths of winter.

Once again, no sound was heard
For an even longer instant,
Something evil then half-stirred
E'er more painful, e'er more distant.

One by one, each frightened soul
Picked at random from the fringe,
Scararossa's death patrol
Ran amok in rage unhinged;

And in the midst of this white lot,
Splattered blood on frosty canvas,
Where, as the circle smaller got,
Vanished hope with raw sadness.

Soon, this state of terse despair
Got to Reytan's vigilance,
Who then bounded up the stairs,
Knowing peril was immense.

"Royal Highness, you must flee."
He burst into the tower on Sass;
"Menace of a savage degree
Is at the gates, flee you must."

"The Knight had previously made plain
That high victory's in our court,
He still has a troops of bairns."
The baffled king did retort.

"I beseech you, waste no time;
Follow me to safety, sir."
Down the stairwell they both climbed
Clutching blindly at cold air.

Reytan led them far below
To the catacombs of death,
Where no brave men e'er dared go,
And even demons held their breaths.

Darkness was silent and sour,
Reytan and the king spoke nowt
For the longest ever hour
Of trepidation, fear, and doubt.

Walls of stone crept all around them,
Cold and mean, yet safe and sound,
The Vilaherts would never find them
In this bygone underground.

Suddenly, a clunk of metal
Echoed through the catacombs,
The doors creaked open to unsettle,
Sass shrieked mildly "Death is soon!"

But in the light of fusty air
That slowly entered in its right,
A beat and bloody, but not scared,
Stood the figure of The Knight.

"Are you here, my overlord?
A piece of cloth I found of yours.
Fear not, no more discord,
The Vilaherts have fled on horse."

Day Eight

"Arise, Sir Duncan, as henceforth thou shalt
be known."
Sass began the day with ceremony,
"Thou art but second to my crown,
Dominant shall be thy hegemony."

The Knight stood haughtily aloft
In the dimly-lit cold throne room,
Dressed in gold-thread tunic, soft
And handsome, swathed in perfume,

Ignorant of Reytan's presence
Though he was their only witness,
Jesters to him were plain peasants,
Courtyard fools and Sass's sickness.

Reytan's hatred and mistrust
Foamed beneath the faint exterior,
Fawn upon the knighthood must
All impecunious inferiors.

He peered outside into the void
Seeing blackness bathed in white,
Feeling desperate to avoid
Piteous arrogance of The Knight.

A numbing wind had now cocooned
The castle walls in every part;
And the freezing winter's brassy Moon
Felt much colder than a preacher's heart.

Every creature of the wilderness
Nestled in its hollow haven,
Birds grew quiet in their stillness
Save the shrieking of one raven;

Treetops howled like ghosts impugned,
Tarns and lakes cracked ice sheet covers,
Huts by stinging frost consumed,
And choking grass with snow was
smothered.

"I'll get men to gather cottonwood."
The Knight broke Reytan's rumination,
Beaming with a new-found statehood
And his master's adulation.

Rode he out the gates with great affront
And a gang of slave enforcers,
Capable of mostly grunts,
Useless in all forms of warfare.

And at the helm, by his side,
Witless Tersius and dumb Gabe,
Crude and crass personified,
Leading this rank cavalcade.

Pretty soon, the desperate minions
Of the realm of Woros slaved,
Gathering wood while crudely pinioned,
Far too weak to show their rage.

Hundred carts of fresh-cut logs
Driven were into the stores,
Tersius beat the underdogs
For he craved that much more.

"Come, you vassals", Gabe opined,
"Deadly winter's come upon us;
Every further branch entwined
Is a small, but worthy bonus."

Men too feeble were despatched
With a sword and a grunt
By The Knight's band of snatches -
Lowlife, dirty, reeking runts.

Finally, when the stores were crammed,
And the people close to dying,
Castle gates were closed and armed,
Leaving them in cold snow lying.

Every bloody frozen eyeball
Peered up at the rampart gates,
Swearing vengeance at the stone walls
Of the royal advocate.

Deep within, the warmth and comfort
Of a sweet and smoky atmosphere
Wafted through the gilded court
Where they dined on fallow deer.

Sass and pompous Knight's two felons
Fell asleep from filthy gluttony,
While high above, the Eagle's talons
Scraped the clouds in pain so sullenly.

Reytan spied the raptor's beak
Chomping at the frozen human waste,
Feeling kinship with this bleak
Bird of prey and of distaste.

Meanwhile, while the vile pigs snored,
Lone Sir Duncan strutted in a ring,
Swinging wildly with his sword,
Telling tall tales to the slumbering king.

The Knight he loved to hear his voice,
It mattered not that no one listened,
Reytan had to, he'd no choice,
Offered he thus no resistance.

He told the tale once more again
Of how he beat the Vilaherts
At their very own cruel game
And how he came out all unhurt,

How Perfidio begged for mercy,
How Scararossa limped away,
How the whole tribe is now nursing
Wounds, and how he made the nomads pay.

Deep into the heavy hour,
Vain Narcissus spoke of fame
And of glory over those that cowered
In the presence of his name.

The king, he woke with a shudder
Halfway through this monologue,
Then back to sleep he recovered,
Slavering like a fat bullfrog.

This sore farce with arrogance imbued
Went on for the longest time,
Broken up by maids with wood
Stoking fires all in line.

Each one bent in adoration
Of this champion of the land,
But underneath, they hid vexation
With tear-filled eyes like gritted sand.

Every living, sentient entity
That had luck to still have life
Loathed The Knight with much intensity
And vowed to end him with a knife.

Reytan's heart was too now warmed
By the flames of these poor maids,
He was too of hardship born,
Knew he why they were afraid.

Jesters duteous had to be
As not bred from royal blood,
Doomed to serve nobility
For their veins they flowed with mud.

Reytan's head was filled with strain,
Just as much as every bone,
Viewed he Sass with much disdain,
And often sat he in his throne;

The sunken eyes within his head
Oft they filled with heavy tears,
Writhing painfully in his bed,
Torturing him for many years.

His breath was shallow, he felt old,
Raw ambition gave to pique,
Sanity was tough to hold
When his brain was so damn sick;

And every sinew of his body
Tried to brush off maidens' smarts.
Best to listen to nobody,
Best to not have a kind heart.

Reytan looked down at the floor
Where a single cockroach roamed,
It must have travelled from the store
When the wood got mixed with corn.

He watched it move out of the shadows
Right into the light of fires
Then crawl across the leather bellows,
Moving like a haunted friar.

'Twas dressed in finest garb of brown,
With the longest pair of whiskers,
Hissing with the meanest sound
Of a rabid, pungent whisper.

And lured by brightness of the blaze,
It got too close to its flame,
Where it stood in awe and daze,
As it caught its legs aflame.

Reytan watched it burn to black,
Without showing any passion,
He could not bring its life force back,
Drained of pity and compassion.

All around him, beauteous beasts
Full of grace and high regard,
While he demanded less than least;
For the cockroach, life was hard.

And all the warmth within his heart
Sank below life's bottom line,
He was dealt the lowest card,
Ever trailing far behind.

The jester curled up by the fire,
For once actually feeling cold,
Looking at this dunce in gold attire,
Feeling worthless, tired, and old.

The Knight now finished his oration,
For the scathing frost had dropped,
The Sun became the land's salvation
And the bitter winds had stopped.

Doors were opened, gates ajar,
Winter quickly gave to springtide;
The air outside near and far
Soon became as warm as inside.

The king had woken from his sleep,
Just in time to trudge to bed,
Reytan looked out of the keep
To see fields of molten dead.

Day Nine

The morning dew had not yet settled
On the rugged Woros plains,
Vapid spirit of dead nettle
Fought for space among henbane

And water hemlock, waterlogged,
Catching breath while drowning so,
Decorating fetid peat bogs
Where the blood would often flow.

Wispy plumes of acrid smoke,
Penetrating clouds of mist,
And all that lived began to choke,
Hoping it could soon desist.

Through the clag came a frail phantom,
Wavering like a cold blue flame,
Floating down the Caitiff's Canyon
Pallid as a whooping crane.

No one noticed it approach,
Guards still drowsy from the night,
Not an invite, not a note,
Through the gates it passed in flight.

It disappeared deep inside
The castle walls without a stir,
To reappear by king's bedside
With no one knowing it was there.

Reytan lightest sleeper was
And always up at break of day;
Heard he but a faint noise
Coming from king's bedroom way.

He hid behind the musty door
Peering in to see what news,
Within, a figure in veil adorned
With runes emblazoned on its shoes.

Sass awoke with a fright
And at the phantom's face he yelled,
Then whispered with a chest most tight
"Aurelia! Have you brought me down to
Hell?"

The sorceress she revealed her greasy head
And hissed with venom like a snake,
"Fear ye not, you're not yet dead,
But your life - it is at stake.

While you have been at your bliss,
You've been betrayed by your shadow,
A Judas sold you with a kiss,
You've been backstabbed by your
bedfellow."

"What say you?" cried the frightened king,
"Who is this deceitful villain
With its scorpion tail that stings?
Tell, Aurelia, I will kill him."

She smiled with many broken teeth
And stroked his sweaty pale blue face,
"You have never peered beneath,
So your trust has been misplaced.

Two strong arms by your flanks,
But which is right and which is left?
Which when speaks is more than frank
And which deceives you to impress?

One has led you up to heavens,
Then through cowardice deceived you,
Second one to hell had taken
You, and safety guaranteed you.

I should gouge your eyes with talons,
For they're useless and you're blind,
How can you judge truest valiance
When you leave your sight behind?

I am warning you", she loomed above,
"Lest your death is sweet to you,
Cut the arm I speak of
Before it turns to strangle you.

When the Sun imbues the sky
With the morning's first bright kiss,
Seek the truth: What, when, why?
And not a single word dismiss."

Sass by then had turned pure white
And pulled the sheets up to his neck,
Riding up the wall to hide
Whilst sinking like a war-torn wreck.

"Am I in midst of nightmare terrors?
Are you an unholy hallucination?
Am I a victim of my deadly errors
Or a creator of my own damnation?"

Aurelia closer to his face got then,
Her odious breath embalmed his mind,
"Remember – truth: what, why, and when?
Your eyes can see now, you're not blind."

With this, she floated 'cross the floor,
Up onto the window's rim,
Then with a swipe, she was no more,
And left the broken monarch grim.

Reytan too slumped into murk,
With his mind running amok,
While the king went half-berserk,
Suffering from delayed shock.

"Only two I've ever trusted,
Only Reytan and The Knight.
Which one is the maladjusted?
Which one's squarely on my side?

How could I have been so lame
In recognising false manoeuvres?
Nothing now will be the same,
I must be rid of fetid tumours."

He donned a cloak of darkest cloth,
And with his eyes still bulging wide,
While trying to show he was not wroth,
Crept soundlessly outside.

Reytan followed him as if a gnat,
Eager to find out what next,
The Knight - he was Aurelia's rat,
But was the king too far perplexed?

Sass came down to handmaids' quarters,
And woke the two that slept the night,
"I come in confidence, your only orders
Are to tell the truth, for it is right.

A ghostly phantom visit gave,
Informed me I have been betrayed,
Speak now, before it is too late,
Speak only truth, my fair handmaids."

"We are in fear", replied the first one,
"We have been tortured for to lie.
Please, sir, please make us certain
That when we tell you, we'll not die."

"Who did this to you?" spoke the king
aghast,
"I guarantee your safety's tight."
The second maiden, head downcast,
Whispered "please, your highness, 'twas The
Knight."

"Why?!" cried the king, "why did he torture
you?!
What made him do such deed?
When? Tell, I order you,
Each grisly detail I shall need."

The first maiden, face full of fear,
Opened her mouth with shallow breath,
"When Vilaherts were throwing spears,
Burning villages, spreading death,

The feeble troops of The Knight
Were wiped out swiftly with one swoop

The bairns he then sent out to fight
Were squashed by Scararossa's troops.

Perfidio rode into our castle courtyard
And swiped The Knight off his horse,
Who begged him then for his own safeguard,
And pleaded he use no more force.

He offered Vilaherts your coffers,
Advised them you were in the keep,
Presented both to them as offer,
So in return his life he'd keep.

The Vilaherts a proud race are, sir,
By chivalry each one is measured,
When Scararossa could not find sir,
Perfidio took just half the treasure.

And as they all rode out the front gates,
He took one last look at The Knight,
And muttered softly with much hate:
'All cowards dress in white.'"

"The scoundrel, the snake within my grass!"
King Sass was gripped by fury,
"He's made of me an ass,
Now I will be his jury.

One of you, fetch my guards,
The other get me Reytan,

And pray avoid the yard,
Lest you should meet that Satan."

Now Reytan he heard this,
So like an owl he scarpered,
Then gathering all his wits,
Back to his bed he started.

It was some time before
The maid she finally came;
She pushed the heavy door
And softly called his name.

"Arise, Reytan, the king he needs you,
Clandestine is this damned affair,
Tell no one when you make it through."
Replied he to her – "I'll be there."

Sass was heavy in his throne
With twelve guards round his person,
The jester entered all alone,
Hearing muffled words of cursing.

"You tried to warn me, my old friend."
The king addressed the fool with gravity,
"I failed to judge and comprehend
The Knight had plunged into depravity,

But I was deaf as well as blind,
His cowardice and rank ineptitude

Has nearly robbed me of my mind
And shook my faith in rectitude."

"What has The Knight been guilty of?"
Feigned Reytan real surprise,
While he removed his threadbare glove
To hide contentment deep inside.

"Like a dog, he ran from Vilaherts,
Then lied to us about his acts,
He gave Perfidio half my gold, for I have
checked,
And tried to sell me too, and that's a fact.

And thanks to him, I have no army,
Nor have I funds left for to arm,
I am now weak and going barmy,
Too weak to not to come to harm."

Reytan listened to the king's tirade,
While gleefully feeling tad amused
How he berated the disloyal renegade
Whom he so recently did use.

Sass had feared for his fate
And for his own reputation,
Not a word about the state
Of his land's impoverished nation.

"Enough brooding!" barked the king,

"Send The Knight to catacombs,
Lock the door and melt the keys,
For long eternity, they will be his tomb."

And from that moment, just plain Duncan
Rotted slowly out of sight,
While Reytan took up his new function
At the facile monarch's side.

Day Ten

It was a sunny morn in Woros,
With verdant mountains gleaming clear,
The eerie sound of the dawn chorus
Was heard first time in years.

Some folk from far off villages
Had started gathering at the hills;
'Twas time to worship icon images
 Of saints who sanction kills.

Inside the royal palace, within Cloth Hall,
Sartorial servants paid lip service
To Reytan as they measured him all
For garments fit for purpose.

He wore pure black, as black as hell,
The finest black of darkest shade
With silver skulls instead of bells
On the fool's cap horns they had just made;

His dress more solemn than a crypt
His chiselled face sharp as a tack,
Black breeches and black shoes with pointed
tips,
Big silver skull sewn into his black back.

He cut a menacing sable figure in this garb,
And even straightened his bent spine;
Who caught his eye would feel disturbed
By movements dark and serpentine.

Power's sacred and the jester knew this well,
Long and torturous's been his path;
Since King Sass had rung The Knight's
death knells,
It's been closer to his grasp.

Skeletal fingers tensed up white
Around the Stygian bauble heart
That formed the sceptre he held tight
To sham a mastery of black arts.

He knew this was his perfect time,
Aurelia did her promised deed,
The Knight paid for his vile crimes,
And Sass removed the toxic weed.

People harboured so much hatred
For the blundering chevalier,
That Reytan could just stand there naked

And still be so much more revered;

He mounted a black stallion,
From Sass this was his prize
For loyalty and duteous valiance,
As well as conduct just and wise.

Then rode he out with a small posse
Of specially chosen men-at-arms
To watch the celebrations while he
Left the gates wide open, so as not to cause
alarm.

He ordered some of his companions
To disperse and ride alone,
Go spread the word that debts and ransoms
Were forbidden from then on.

He instructed them to show compassion
In the face of hardship's pique,
To offer access to king's rations,
Feed the hungry, cure the weak,

To be fluid in their promises,
And to ooze transparency,
To speak honestly on their policies
And be upright through sincerity,

To inspire to be virtuous,
To be humble and demure,

To be shrewd, but not tempestuous,
To be lucid, firm, and pure.

Many had now come to Reytan,
Granting their sky-high respects,
Every village had priests waiting,
Offering canons of blest texts.

Growing was his grand repute
With each liberal noble gesture,
So calculating and astute
Was he in his pre-planned venture.

He knew damn well that Sass was deaf
To what his subjects longed to speak,
Of hope and love they were bereft,
Their future twisted and oblique.

He knew that preachers show their best
Through practice of the words they utter,
And that people most oppressed
Are by and large the ones that chiefly matter.

He shook their hands tight and firm,
And spoke with softness and faux modesty,
He feigned concern at every turn
And signalled virtues with dishonesty;

A paragon of righteousness,
A model of celestial morality,

They sang to him, "Come enlighten us,
Oh, Reytan, champion of vitality."

And one by one, they paid respects
To the angel of the dark
Till the jester's intellect
And perseverance made its mark.

He rode through crowds of hungry folk,
Proudly strutting on his horse,
Grinning at his masterstroke
Of wholly lifting The Knight's curse.

His head was clouded by the clamour
Of the masses in their praise,
So he did not notice in the drama
That his steed had gone its wayward way.

Suddenly, the forest overtook him,
Where no soul was to be seen,
And everywhere he started looking
Emptiness felt stark and mean;

Birds had stopped their gossip too,
And leaves on trees now failed to stir,
Stillness stunned as silence grew
In dingy darkness everywhere.

All at once, the shuddering panic
That his mind had settled into

Gave way to dread e'er more frantic
In the menace that ensued.

He had never knowed such silence
And his pounding heart had told him so;
Smothering, deadening, noiseless violence
Of this lonely void of woe.

He commanded his dark stallion
To go forth straight ahead,
Only to be met by one more alley
With an end that was as dead.

East was West, and North was South,
Only clouds obscured the sky,
Blackness opened its foul mouth
And swallowed remnants of daylight.

Reytan stood now motionless
In the middle of this vacuum,
His sword held tight against his chest,
Consumed by cold blood-curdling gloom.

He could not move, nor would he want to,
For fear of dying of fear of death,
His face had turned a shade of sour blue
From holding on to shallow breath.

Then through this weight of horrid silence,
Faint bleak whispers came within

Like a song of slaughtered sirens,
Pulling at his frozen skin:

"Reytan, Reytan, we can see you,
We can see what's in your soul,
You can't fool us, we're within you,
We know every lie you've told."

"Damn be gone!", he cried to them,
Though not sure which way to speak;
His mind was growing more confused and
Body started to feel weak.

"Reytan, Reytan, we are watching
Every time you feign goodwill,
You speak kindness, all while plotting
How to perpetrate your next kill."

"Spirits of the forest, please,
Do not torture me this cruel way,
I am pleading on my knees."
He replied in disarray.

"Reytan, Reytan, you're a shicer,
Mountebank and charlatan,
A self-serving scam deviser,
Scheming coward of a man."

"What say you?!" he gave to wrath,
"The Knight was worst at conjuring sins!"

The ghostly voices up the path
Whispered back: "You're worse than him."

Reytan slumped onto the ground,
Clutching at his broken heart,
Screaming agony with no sound,
Anger tearing him apart.

Clouds above him turned to black,
Swirling darkness mangled fierce,
Pushing down his twisted back
Till his mouth had tasted earth.

Motionless he lay till night,
Dead inside, numb and empty,
High above - two bright eyes
Of the Eagle watching him intently.

Day Eleven

Reytan opened his red eyes,
Trying to make sense through the stupor
Of the rumbling in his mind
And the stench of Hades sewers;

The sky above him, dense and choking,
Swayed with much unease,
Dust like sleet within it floating
Tasted bitter of disease.

He picked himself up off the ground
Slowly, so he'd mask the constant pain,
Carefully prodding all around
With a makeshift wooden cane.

He could hear the frightened horse
Whinnying somewhere close nearby,
So he dragged himself to it perforce
And grabbed the bridle with a cry.

And with what strength he had remaining,
Mounted it he then swiftly,
In the distance, winds were wailing
With plumes of acrid dust grains drifting.

The rumbling had got louder then,
And air got even thicker still,
Reytan bolted back to Sass's den
Past the quaking of the hills.

"People, people, get your wares,
Seize your loved ones and your kin,
Don't get caught unawares,
Run to caves and stay within!

There's no time now, move you quick,
Stall you now, regret you later,
Clouds of ash will rain thick
From the spewing of the crater!

Guards shall fetch the king and court,
Servants, priests, and courtesans,
Cattle, poultry, pigs, and transport,
And there'll be no favouring none;

Follow me now all to shelter,
Caves of Mortal Sin are vast,
Move! Don't wait for the crater
To claim victory, run now fast!"

Reytan's frenzied pleading worked;
Soon the king and all his subjects
Fled to caves to hide in dark,
Fearing happenstance most abject.

Food was justly distributed,
Blankets given to all frail,
Fires lit and barefoot booted,
Thirsty given were warm ale.

And while the king sat chewing nettles,
Jester's servants made the rounds,
Making sure the beasts were settled
And no one ventured out of bounds.

They did not have to wait that long
For the boom to shake the land;
Reytan right was all along -
Ground exploded with a bang.

Saffron fluid lava flowed
Up into the blood red sky,
Fiery air with anger glowed,
All without would melt and fry.

Magma fissured from the vents,
And everywhere chunks of tephra
Littered the surrounding land,
Blown around by winds of Zephyr.

Clouds of ash thrown to the skies
Fell onto the ground like snow,
Suffocating rats and flies
And anything it caught below.

The heat was palpable in the caves,
And people moved within to cool;
It came to burn the skin in waves,
Such is nature at most cruel.

Reytan brought up pails of water
From the depths of lowest caverns
To the ones that felt the hottest
In a most pensive manner.

And while his servants carried on
Tending to those most affected,
He walked up to the makeshift throne
And offered Sass his own perspective:

"Your royal highness, we need wait
For the anger of the gods to pass,
We have plenty food to fill our plates
And enough water for to last."

Sass looked bored, then he stopped chewing
The dead nettle's rigid stems,
His fair maids were busy brewing
Cold mud tea, which they only served to
men;

He looked at Reytan with disdain,
"You dragged us here, sure 'twas wise,
But the scorching air brings pain,
And the floor's not civilised.

How can I make regal judgements
In an atmosphere of such bedlam,
Of an odour e'er so pungent,
And of noise e'er so deafening?

Come, my friend, hand me succour
On a plate instead of food,
Serve me portions of grand valour,
Bring me solace, lift my mood."

Reytan's bony fingers tightened round his
sword,
His firmly grounded feet then gave a
noiseless twitch,
He felt a bellow coming on, but said no
word,
Angry that the king's throat was just out of
reach.

He drew a breath to steady nerves,
And composed himself with a wry smile:
"Sir, our flock we must preserve,
We may be here for a while."

Sass removed his line of sight

To focus on the mud tea maid,
"We best not be here till midnight,
Early eve will be too late."

The jester took a painful bow,
Gritting at his grubby teeth,
Desperate not to let it show
He was livid underneath.

He spent the next few restless hours
Pacing up and down the mouths of caves,
Peering at the ashen showers
Pouring down on Woros plains.

Then he sat himself by the rim,
Overlooking the apocalypse,
Looking gaunt, sick, tired, and thin,
Muttering weakly through his lips:

"What is life if not a journey,
One without a destination?
Why does this vile thought concern me,
When I'm in need of consolation?

Is my anger aimed at kings
Or at voices of pure conscience in my head?
Do I covet love, fame, or mere temporal
things?
Do I fear my time of death, or just the
thought of being dead?

Life's a struggle, one that does not reap
rewards,
You jump onto it in midstream
As it's galloping towards
An ever more retreating dream.

Oftentimes I've been a fool,
And placed my feet at evil's door,
But loyalty is a tool
That the devil frequently chooses to ignore.

The bitter feed my soul consumes
Comes not from him but my own angst;
This poison smells like sweet perfume,
And I drink it from my own hands.

Just what does it take to prove your worth
When you're never even seen,
In the shadows since your birth,
Always stuck in-between?

Noblemen move the quill
That writes the history of life's woes,
Then knock the ink well so it spills
Onto the pages in mid flow.

And I am nothing but soiled vermin
Gnawing on their wooden door,
While inside the screw is turning
To keep it locked forever more.

I cannot feel for numbness that oft dulls me,
I cannot think for chaos in my brain,
I cannot see while my aspirations blind me,
Nor can I move because I'm lame.

So here I ask of no one but myself -
What is life's most torrid feud?
Is it the conflict that's within ourselves
Or the battle between all evil and all good?"

Reytan's broken, cast-down figure
Threw a shadow on the rock behind him,
Crisp and spearlike, like a pillar
In the darkness of surroundings.

His breath stood still, his eyes were glazed,
He blew the air with one great puff,
Then knocked himself out of his daze
With a wild howl, most pained and gruff.

Outside, the fields of spelt were calmer now,
And everywhere blue smoke it drifted low,
What once was crass and mean, and loud
Had only strength enough to faintly glow.

So Reytan stood, then slowly ambled
Down to where the king had sat,
Addressed him, e'er low and humble,
Without removing his black cap:

"Sire, the worse it seems is now behind,
The gods have given us some welcome
respite,
If it shall please your royal mind,
I'll ride without to test the site."

Sass threw up a withering arm,
And mumbled something no one heard.
"When I am sure that we are safe from harm,
I shall ride back", Reytan declared.

Heavy silver skulls they jangled,
The black rider on his steed went far
Into the land where trees laid mangled,
Embedded in fresh layers of char.

He slowly moved across the land
Testing ground for sturdy strength,
But most fields were like bowls of fine sand
Across its breadth and length.

And just as he was poised to turn,
He spied a lonely figure standing still
Looking ghostlike, mean, and stern,
'Neath the next abandoned hill.

He neared to it and gave a start,
Aurelia 'twas and she looked glum.
"What now, oh blackened heart?
 Where to, oh devil's son?"

She spat these words with venom spit,
Like a horned viper in attack,
"You still owe me, don't forget.
We once had made a pact.

The gods are mad!" she hissed at Reytan,
"They are but nature's love and fury."
Exclaimed he, "I am not Satan.
They're not my judge and jury."

"You're still a heathen and a skunk,
Your heart and mind as black as coal,
My nettle confit stew you drank,
Soon I will have your murky soul."

Then suddenly, she snarled and turned
To disappear deep into the fog,
While Reytan saw the king returning
Through the fields with his whole flock.

Above the land, a screech was heard,
The Eagle of Demise was near,
It screamed at every raven bird,
And people stopped in frozen fear.

It wasn't long before entire clouds
Of sable birds had gathered high,
Then hurled themselves onto the crowds
Each with its own war cry.

The king was first to castle walls
And closed the gates fast behind;
Reytan clung onto his horse
And swung his sword a hundred times.

He fought the hungry raven mass
With every ounce of sinewed bone,
Mad with fury that King Sass
Left him out here all alone.

Finally, heavily bloodied and half-dying,
He slipped onto a secret path
Which led into an old, abandoned mine.
There, he waited for the aftermath.

He saw children, men, and wives
Being ravaged by the swarm,
He saw many lose their lives
While King Sass sat in the warm.

High above, the Eagle hollered
Seething with a wrath untold;
Deep within his broken soul,
Reytan now felt hollow, bitter, blue, and
cold.

Day Twelve

With morning dew a shade of crimson,
And brazen smoke that spun and billowed,
The remnant breaths of the dominion
Fell deep into the earth's soft pillow.

The Sun cut wounds like a thin sheet of
metal
Into the bodies that now lay in rest
Throughout the land devoid of any mettle,
With treachery embedded in its sunken
chest.

Whether 'twas famine, plague, or war,
All conspired in one fell swoop
To twist the knife into its core
For death to serve its cynical rebuke.

Somewhere else, life flourished,
But here the end was now in sight;
All dreams and visions, hungry and
malnourished,

Perished ere the morning light.

The black figure of the breathless jester
Sat up in agony with blood trickling down
Onto the silver skulls of his cap, once
majestic,
Now torn and crumpled half off his crown.

With crackle in his lungs and lesions on his
arms,
He stood up with a pained woeful wail,
Then turned he his dry eyes to scan
The land around him whilst struggling to
inhale.

His sword still firmly clenched
By his stiffened and numb hand,
In his and dead raven blood drenched,
Poised to defend till the end.

He walked slowly through the emptiness
before him,
Watching for signs of any mere life,
But everywhere, silence was calling,
Pierced by rough winds, which still have not
died.

Half-frozen mud creaked 'neath his boots,
The stench of rot made him feel sick,
He walked mile after mile o'er tree roots

That kept the mud firm and thick.

Nothing and then more horrid nothing,
Though he could hear some faint moaning
somewhere,
He pointed t'wards it for something
To come at him through the air.

He finally spotted some folk,
Writhing in pain on the ground,
So covered he one with his own cloak
And next to him then he crouched down.

"Reytan", the man spoke with low strength,
"Save us from tyranny, neglect, and
oppression.
You've been born from our depths,
You're one of us, you're our salvation.

You've been sent by the gods
To grant protection from King Sass,
To spare us the beats of his rod,
Save us, our brother, you must."

"I'm not who thou think'st I am,
And neither whom I see in looking-glass."
Mouthed this Reytan at the dying man,
Whose breaths were now fading fast.

"No selfless deed has e'er come from me,

I've paved my path with the dead,
Yet still I see more walls before me,
And lines of them straight up ahead.

We peasants, servants, and serfs,
Can ne'r be free from these masters of greed,
Lest we become them ourselves,
And copy them in every foul deed.

A cockroach like me with ambition,
Seeking fame, strength, love, or glory,
Gets burnt in the fires of perdition,
When the gods get bear of its story."

Reytan peered at the corpse near his feet,
Then looked up to the welkin for riposte,
His anger was now complete,
And faith in his choices all lost.

He started to yell and to howl,
And swung his cracked sword at the air,
Then stabbed the ground with a growl,
And pulled at his blood-matted hair.

He set out towards the castle gates,
Scowling, sneering, and spitting about,
Hollering with much hostility and hate,
Blood dripping from his crooked mouth.

Soon, his black and red figure appeared

At the courtyard of imperial decay,
He searched long and hard, yet none was
near,
From the bell-tower down to the ruined
causeway.

He then sneaked inside the royal chambers.
Careful not to make one audible sound,
And deep within the throne room, there
He saw King Sass adjusting his dirty gold
crown.

All around him were jewels and more gold,
Strewn across the filthy cold stone floor,
Mixed in with discarded bones and mould,
All the way up to the back door

Where Reytan stood in smouldering stupor:
The king had gathered his last wealth,
And feasted in its dirt no sooner
Than when his land had lost its health.

On each of the two stately seats
Sat Tersius and Gabe from the Knight's
crew,
Servile to Sass since Duncan's defeat,
Sticking to him like hot glue.

"Friends", the king spoke unto them,
"Vast is my realm of plentitude

106

And lustrous is my jewelled diadem;
Thus to show my humble gratitude,

I make you my Guards of Honour.
E'er since that Reytan leech,
Good-for-no one puny fawner,
Had abandoned me in dire need,

You've shown me such servitude,
And principled loyalty to the crown.
I place my trust in your good,
Knowing you shall not let me down.

When the Sun sets at night,
Go and find a fair few maids,
For those that served before have died.
Tell them they will get much paid."

"Glad to, sire", exclaimed Tersius,
"We shall do as you desire."
He winked at Gabe with a grin most heinous
And threw some bones onto the fire.

"Let us dine some more, your royal
highness,
We shall fetch another trough,
And then celebrate your sterling kindness
Till the Moon stays still aloft."

With this, the two stolid men

Got up and walked out through the front
door,
While Sass perused his filthy, squalid den
And grasped his royal livery collar off the
floor.

He placed the heavy chain round his bulging
neck,
And sat admiring how it made him glow,
Picking off each microscopic speck
Of dust that settled on his mantle cloak of
indigo.

Reytan's eyes were piercing the foul air,
His stare so still it froze all time,
The moment was preserved everywhere,
His thoughts committed now to grandest
crime.

He lunged owl-like onto Sass,
And clutched the bulky chain with both his
hands,
Then yanked it with all strength he's ever
had
To pull the gasping king into death's
shadowland;

He strained his every sinew and nerve
Till his knuckles turned blue grey,
Hissing madly with much verve,

Draining the fat man's life away

Till one final hoarse long breath
Echoed through the vacant space,
And one more being met its death,
This time with a royal face.

Reytan stepped back in mild shock
To see the outcome of his art,
Dazed as if he had sleepwalked,
Feeling crude awareness in his heart.

"Sass is dead, of that I'm sure,
But what of fear of consequence?
Was my deed premature
Or inevitable circumstance?

Who is here to view this now
When all round are sleeping dead?
What I've done I'll disavow
If I'm judged by just my head.

Tersius, Gabe, they will be back,
And this body will go sour,
Best that I be making tracks
In a fraction of this hour."

Reytan ran out like a man possessed
Into vastness of the day,
Heading into winds northwest,

Hoping to get far away.

Heard he horses galloping behind,
As he tried to swiftly flee,
And as he turned to ease his mind,
He saw that there were none but three.

He jumped ahead for safety's sake,
But suddenly one gripped him tight,
He thought he must have made mistake
When he saw it was The Knight.

"You rag-dirty scoundrel parasite!"
Barked Sir Duncan with a sneer,
While Tersius and Gabe used their might
To trap Reytan with their spears.

They all pounced on him with zest,
And by now he had no strength left,
Tersius sat upon his broken chest,
Gabe took care of all the rest.

The Knight stood proud above his prey,
And threw his chin up to the sky.
"You've assumed I'd rot away
Or perhaps take leave to die,

But these two fine gentlemen
That are sitting on your carcass
Hid me, fed me, freed me then,

While King Sass was in the darkness.

And now you gave me the best gift,
Getting rid of that fat fool,
The winds of change will smoothly shift
And I shall take his place of rule."

With this he got the two turncoats
To tie up Reytan with a heavy chain
To the martyr post, where only days ago
The royal hearse-monger died in so much
pain.

And as they started back to fort,
The Knight he turned upon his horse:
"You've lost your case in nature's court,
You cannot fight against its force."

Reytan looked at the three figures
Moving steadily towards horizon,
His stature ever more disfigured,
As he watched the halfmoon rising.

In the distance he could spy
A pair of eyes that showed no hatred,
The Eagle of Demise refused to fly,
It now looked tired of life and jaded.

Day Thirteen

In the desolate and deserted landscape
Of the twilight of this morn,
Where once stood a row of mandrake,
Bordered by the fields of wheat and corn,

Where the sheep and cattle grazed
And the herds of sable horses
By the serfs were duly raised
For the nation's defence forces,

Stood just one abandoned post,
High upon a flattened plateau,
Where - wrapped round as if a ghost
Reytan slumped was in his shadow.

He lifted up his heavy head
And squirmed around to loosen chains,
With blood dried up to rust-brown red
And crusted up to numb the pain.

He felt the gentle winds upon his face,
But could not sense from whence they came;
The land around him was bare space,
With all directions much the same.

He was devoid of any thought,
Nor was there point in starting one,
No single word did leave his throat,
He could not speak it to no one.

Not far away and in plain sight,
And watching him in peaceful candour,
Was the Eagle of Demise
With eyes of shimmering golden amber.

Near him, an unkindness of black ravens,
Pacing up and down the earthy mesa:
A masterpiece of Reytan's cadence
Played upon the death's oasis.

A man cannot be limited by fate
If it's been of his design,
Every waking hour's too late
In the playground of one's time,

Yet somehow all eternity
'S not enough to cast rogue cards,
For in the annals of humanity
Nature favours the diehards.

Reytan stared into the distant light
Where rolling clouds of mist ran free,
Studying smoky wisps of dirty white
Moving through the barren lea.

He watched this flight of nature's solitude
All tied up in fancy knots,
Then squinted eyes as best he could,
For suddenly, he thought he spied a small
red dot.

At first dreamed he it was his eyes
In failing mind's imagination fecund,
But then the dot had started to materialise
As it got bigger each and every second.

Like a vision of impending doom,
The small red dot took on a concrete shape,
And just past the striking of the noon
Emerged out of the bleakness of landscape.

The horse was sinewed, firm just like a
statue,
The rider even more so, and both dressed in
red,
Reytan looked at this imposing view
Of Scararossa with a tilted head.

Many had feared this ruthless warrior,
Slaughter followed him like plague,

Not since time immemorial
Has death been steeped in so much rage.

But Scararossa was not here to maim,
That was plain as he did then dismount,
He showed no anger nor disdain
And placed his sword flat on the ground.

"Reytan, squire, hallowed it will be thy
name,"
Started he with a coarse voice,
"I come to free you from these chains,
This is Perfidio's choice."

The jester took a long, yet shallow breath,
And turned to face the beast in red,
"Pray, why deny me easy death?
Doth he not wish me dead?"

"The Vilaherts are proud in honour
For all who show stark brazen bravery;
Alas, the realm of Woros and enclosures
Was once treacherous and unsavoury.

Its king was futile and unavailing,
Army aimless and decrepit,
People selfish, dim, and failing,
And its faith in humankindness tepid.

You, my squire, showed rare wisdom

Nurturing hope for better futures,
You then dared to buck that system,
Planting seeds of revolution.

But gods had sanctioned the land's torture,
For mere penance was too wan,
And charged the beasts as their enforcers
Till the line of ruin was drawn."

"Yet now tell me, Scararossa, what of
nature's honest people?
Did it fail to keep 'em safe?"
"As is my witness this 'ere bold Eagle,
 They're all within their dark and shallow
graves,

Every noble, slave, and serf,
Mad King Sass and his crew,
Tersius, Gabe, and The Knight himself,
Who told Perfidio all 'bout you;

That grimy coward died a death
Of a thousand bone-deep cuts,
While them two were caught draggin' a chest
Full of royal treasure, the dirty cheating
sewer rats.

Nothing left, none but you,
All the sinners left this place,
Woros is an empty pew,

Empty of its former foul and rotting race."

"But what is one's noble deed
If it cannot free the meek,
If it fails to meet the needs
Of the humble and the weak?

And what's the point of noble victories
When there's no one to share triumphs
Of redemption from iniquities?
I cannot partake in such connivance."

"Said Perfidio he will let your light shine
In the brightest pastures far from Woros,
But he cannot turn back time,
Only future's guaranteed before us."

"Then leave me here just to myself,
For I'm no good to no one now,
My heart and mind my bankrupt wealth,
And death my goal, I here avow.

Pray tell Perfidio I am done,
That I'll be ash in my homeland."
"Aye, squire, your words' tenor I
comprehend,
Your wish will be my just command."

So Scararossa took his sword
And placed it in his crimson scabbard,

Then without saying one more word,
He bowed to Reytan in most modest manner.

Mounted he his faithful horse,
And started riding t'wards horizon -
The blurry soup of sour remorse
Where clouds of rust were now fast rising.

Soon he turned into a dot,
Red and bright against the sky,
And Reytan left was on his spot,
Still tied up in chains so tight.

"I was born of dirt and dust,
Soon I will be that once more,
Then I shall be free at last,
Having won my inner war.

Pointless is each heavy battle,
Worthless is a man's vast wealth,
When in dying breath's death rattle
He can't even save himself.

Take this body, gods above,
Take my cloth and take my name,
Take my vain attempts at love,
Abject failures, and my pain!"

He then slid right to the ground,
To the bottom of the post,

Eyelids slowly shutting down
Till he was but just a ghost.

And all the birds had gathered close,
In half-circle round his corpse,
Ravens, blackbirds, rooks, and crows,
Birds of prey, black-winged storks,

And the Eagle of Demise,
Who was watching from the side,
Let a scream out to the skies
To decry that Reytan's died.

Far across the barren land,
The wail had echoed through the vales,
Right down to the dunes of sand,
Where the sea met crags of shale.

Months had rolled and turned to years,
No more clouds through Woros passed,
The Sun had blessed it with its sphere
And the winds died down at last.

In the gargoyle, sinuous west,
On a mountain bare in bloom,
The Eagle of Demise slept in its hispid nest,
Underneath the midnight Moon.

It woke to meet its faithful owner,
When she brought its daily feed,

Aurelia entered its enclosure
And placed some sea-shrew at its feet.

She stroked its head with gentle motion,
And whispered something in its ear,
The bird repaid her with emotion
And shed a melancholy tear.

Aurelia walked up to the ragged scarp
And peered above the chaparral;
She placed her hand beneath her scarf
And clutched a gleaming silver skull.

Epilogue

Blithely drunken in its verdant haze,
A flurry of soft golden leaves drifts out from
summer air
Through each autumn's brand-new poignant
phase
To then expose the spirit of the winter's fair.

And every morning's daybreak song
Breaks the silence of its grim and ancient
night,
To wake the hyacinths that ere had been
withdrawn
So they can seek the midday of Sun's light.

Each second speaks volumes of its timeless
wealth,
And every living thing embraces its own
fortune,
The veins that run through this here fertile
earth

Are pumping the most pure of nature's
potions.

Life finds the straightest geodesic
To aim at aspirations of a simplest hue,
Its goals are not in character malefic,
Its paths are squarely pure and true.

And if a traveller were to pass here one day,
They would not know its history hiding in
plain sight
Lest they encountered some dark byway
Of Stygian dykes of thicket with no light.

They would not hear the screams
Of hungry masses that got slain,
They would not see the broken dreams
Of those who only knew life's pain,

They would not know the nature's angriest
rage
Beating their backs with sturdiest rods,
Or feel the hopelessness at every stage
That drew no consolation from their own
gods.

Where now on blue-green canvas
Colours glow on wings of dragonflies,
Once roamed dark-spirited and blood-thirsty
bandits,

Collecting worthless treasures and
unfulfilled lives.

It's for the best that truth stays obscured
For it should never be repeated thus,
So let the reader be assured
That truth this cruel must stay forever in the
past.

Let there never be a doubt that life
Cannot be without some minor irritation,
But when pain's jagged knife twists so high
and wide,
It meets the inner mind's inevitable ablation.

It gets forgotten, and yes that's just,
For what pained soul aims to remember?
It floats back down to turn to dust
From whence it came to be engendered.

The flowers that grow within the foliate
grass
Smile deep into your eyes with genuine zeal,
They thrive on now forgotten tales of loss
For years have given them due time to heal.

And new pastures have now grown
With fresh waters flowing through,
Past every smooth, moss-covered stone
Beneath the sky of azure blue.

Yes, now against all odds
The past's been lost and forsaken
Gone are the callous, futile gods,
Gone is the wrath of vulgar Satan,

All gone except the tale that grips
The tongues of curious human creatures,
The legend that shall ne'er take sleep
As it's passed on from teacher to teacher,

The legend of the man that they called
Reytan.

Author's Notes

Aurelia (awe-**rel**-yah)

A sorceress and a soothsayer, she lives alone
in a dilapidated wooden hut by the seafront
in the rugged wilderness west of Woros.
Aurelia knows Reytan is immune to her
threats, unlike King Sass, who fears her and
her witchcraft with much dread. She also
retains an almost god-like reputation among
the illiterate population of Woros and
consequently fears nothing and no one.

Eagle of Demise

A harbinger of doom, which appears
ominously in the skies before each tragedy
that befalls the people of Woros. Its large
and menacing stature instils great fear in
anyone that dares to look at it.

Gabe (geyb)

One of the merciless thugs from The
Knight's gang. Mindless and subservient,
perfect for The Knight's needs.

King Sass (king-**sas**)

Self-serving, shallow, greedy, and ignorant, Sass is a reluctant tyrant through sheer laziness. He views Reytan as wise and useful, but keeps him at a comfortable distance due to the jester's lower class heritage. On the other hand, The Knight is the fawning noble who satisfies the basest need for glorification in Sass, which he gets from him without needing to expend any effort. Sass's survival instincts extend to himself only, so he cares nothing for his people, his kingdom, and indeed his friends beyond what is beneficial to him.

Apparently well educated, yet unable to grasp the gravity of the consequences of his misrule, or even the obvious mistrust of his own subjects. As long as he feels satiated and comfortable, all else pales into significance in his blinkered and shallow world.

Perfidio (per-**fid**-yoh)

The magnanimous, strong, brave, and well-respected leader of the Vilaherts. He has led them on their many epic perilous journeys, and has gained a fearsome reputation across the land. He has trained Scararossa in the ways of war and survival, and trusts him absolutely.

Reytan (ray-tan)

Thrust into servitude to the king as his court jester on the account of his father having done the same job before him, Reytan is frustrated by the arrogance, pomposity, and ineptitude exhibited by the nobles of the court, and in particular King Sass and The Knight. He feels that he could extend his influence over royal decision making and improve the fate of the nation of Woros if only The Knight's importance could be reduced. However, with time he realises that the king will never accept him as an equal owing to his peasant background. Reytan is also constantly torn between satisfying his own greed for power and doing morally righteous and just deeds, and as a result is plagued by self-doubt and debilitating depression.

His mind is unforgivingly dark, yet crystal clear at the same time. His body is strong and sinewy, but twisted and warped – a perfect reflection of his pained and tortured soul. He shows a powerful presence nevertheless, and the impoverished people of Woros worship and adore him as one of their own. There is some uneasy history between him and Aurelia with whom he retains a love-hate relationship, and it is clear that although she would never openly admit it, she is fascinated by his gloomy and mysterious character and nurtures a great deal of respect for him. Scararossa and Perfidio both admire his apparent resolve and wisdom too.

The only person who truly detests and mistrusts Reytan is Reytan himself and his fragile mind suffers immeasurably as a result.

Scararossa (ska-ra-**ro**-sa)

Adopted by Perfidio after the death of his mother at a very young age, Scararossa is meticulously loyal to him, and values courage and military discipline above all other human traits. He is ruthless, vicious, insatiable, and at times known to be dangerously unstable. As a consequence, he is feared by all who have ever had the misfortune to encounter him.

More than that, his formidable reputation precedes him and the bravest warriors tremble at the sound of his name alone.

Tersius (ter-sius)

Gabe's tall and lanky friend, and another thug from The Knight's gang. Greedy, but easily satisfied.

The Knight/Sir Duncan

Born into nobility and Sass's childhood friend, he has become the king's right-hand man and closest confidante by default. Although universally known as The Knight, at first he is not truly a legitimate knight until he is officially knighted after the apparent defeat of the Vilaherts. The people of Woros despise him and fear his destructive influence, along with his band of hand-picked mindless thugs.

He is superficially handsome, well-built, clean-shaven, and always immaculately dressed, but utterly devoid of any real courage, loyalty, or even a smattering of charm. Worse still, he is stolid and ineffective as a military leader, although

Sass is completely blind to all these obvious
shortcomings.

Vilaherts (**vil**-a-herts)

A nomad tribe of warriors, renowned for
their courage and ruthlessness. Although
their fighting skills are feared throughout the
land, they are also highly respected for their
code of chivalry and sense of moral justice.

Woros (**war**-os)

The realm of Woros is hidden in the barren
and rocky lands of a medieval wilderness,
relatively close to the coast where Aurelia
lives.
Its poorer masses are corrupt, selfish, and
uneducated, living in fear of its heartless
king and his incompetent crew of
accomplices. They regard Reytan as their
unofficial representative and champion, and
rather foolishly as a possible saviour from
the tyranny of the rich oppressors residing in
the court of King Sass.
The Vilaherts view Woros as a hub of
immorality and decadence, and its entire
populace as equally evil. All except Reytan,
in whom they see a struggle for good.

Printed in Great Britain
by Amazon